CAPTAIN FACT's

EGYPTIAN ADVENTURE

BY
KNIFE & PACKER

EGMONT

by Egmo   V8 6SA

Printed and bound in Great Britain

CONTENTS

STAR

CLIFF THORNHILL
TV'S WORST WEATHERMAN.

PUDDLES
THE ONLY
WEATHERDOG ON TV.

CAPTAIN FACT
THE WORLD'S FIRST
INFORMATION SUPERHERO.

KNOWLEDGE
CAPTAIN FACT'S
FAITHFUL SIDEKICK.

RiNG...

LUCY
HEAD OF MAKE-UP AND CLIFF'S BEST FRIEND.

THE BOSS
HE'S SCARY!

PROFESSOR MINISCULE
HEAD OF THE FACT CAVE AND THE BRAINS BEHIND MISSIONS.

FACTORELLA
PROFESSOR MINISCULE'S DAUGHTER AND ALL-ROUND WHIZZ-KID.

CHAPTER I
ARCHAEOLOGIST IN DEEP. . .

TV'S WORST WEATHERMAN, Cliff Thornhill, and his co-presenter, Puddles the dog, hadn't had a day off work for ages. So they were really excited to be out of the office and going to the City Museum.

'What a stroke of luck that our day off coincided with a talk from the world's most famous archaeologist,' said Cliff. 'These are the hottest tickets in town! Sir Ramsbottom Tickell's been in Egypt and he's made some amazing discoveries.'

But there was only one thing spoiling their perfect day . . . the Boss had decided to tag along too.

'What's the Boss doing here?' whispered Puddles, who had to keep his voice down when other people were about.

'He must have seen the invitations on my desk,' said Cliff, as they took their seats in the auditorium and awaited the arrival of Sir Ramsbottom.

'He's always snooping,' said Puddles. 'Just last week I'm sure he was sniffing around my liquorice-flavoured dog biscuits.'

Around them the crowd was getting restless: there was no sign of the celebrity archaeologist.

'Strange,' thought Cliff. 'Sir Ramsbottom's never been late for anything in his life.'

'THORNHILL!' shouted the Boss. 'WHAT'S GOING ON? WHERE'S THIS ARCHAEOLOGIST OF YOURS?!'

'Well, er, um, I'm sure he'll be here any minute,' stuttered Cliff. 'He's probably just dusting down a mummy and . . . er . . . polishing up his speech.'

Just then the doors of the auditorium burst open . . . it was Lucy, Cliff's friend from the Make-up Department.

'WHAT ARE YOU DOING HERE?' screamed the Boss. 'I DON'T REMEMBER GIVING YOU THE DAY OFF!'

'Haven't you heard the news?' panted Lucy. 'Sir Ramsbottom's gone missing – lost in the Great Pyramid!'

'LOST IN A PYRAMID?' exclaimed the Boss.

'Yes! He discovered a secret passage into the Great Pyramid,' said Lucy. 'Trouble is, he hasn't been able to find his way back out. Now he's trapped in the pyramid and completely out of contact.'

'I smell a BIG STORY!' shouted the Boss. 'Everyone back to the office NOW! That includes you, Thornhill, and your mutt. I've just cancelled your day off!'

As they charged back to the office, Lucy explained the situation. 'Rescue teams have tried everything, but they just can't find him. Sir Ramsbottom is the only person alive who knew about the secret entrance!'

When they got back to the studio Cliff and Puddles slipped off to their office. 'Strange,' thought Lucy, 'Sir Ramsbottom is Cliff's hero. I thought he'd be more concerned. How can he think about the weather at a time like this?'

As soon as the door shut, Cliff turned to Puddles.

'Well, you know what this means, Puddles?'

'We've had our day off ruined by an archaeologist with a bad sense of direction,' grumbled Puddles. 'I told you we should have gone to the new canine theme park, Doggie Land. They've just opened the Bones of Fire Ride.'

'Don't be ridiculous, Puddles,' said Cliff. 'THIS IS A MISSION FOR CAPTAIN FACT!' and with that he pulled the lever to reveal the entrance to the Fact Cave . . .

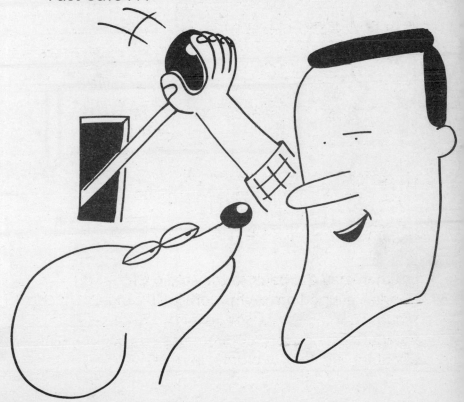

FACT CAVE

'We've got to get to that pyramid as soon as possible,' puffed Captain Fact as they ran up the Fact Cave corridors. 'Sir Ramsbottom will be running out of air.'

'Why doesn't he just follow the exit signs in the pyramid?' asked Knowledge. 'Or use the lift?'

NERVE CENTRE

'Exit signs?
Lifts?' said Captain Fact.
'The whole point of the pyramids
was to keep people out and, if you did
sneak in, to make sure you stayed in!'
And with that his mask
began to wiggle . . .

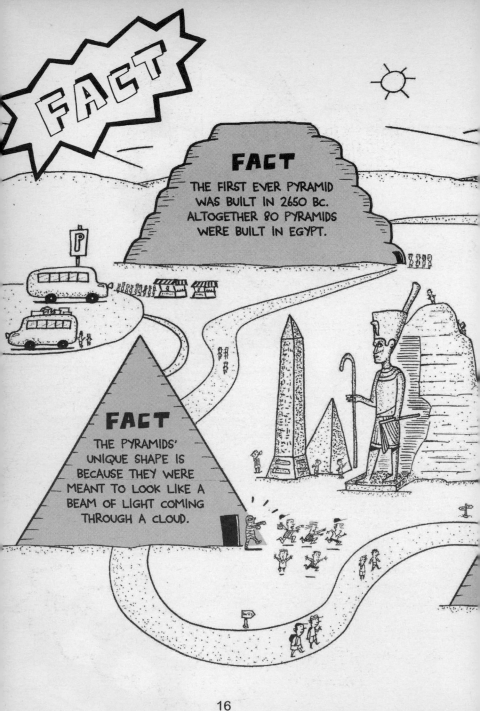

FACT

FACT
THE FIRST EVER PYRAMID
WAS BUILT IN 2650 BC.
ALTOGETHER 80 PYRAMIDS
WERE BUILT IN EGYPT.

FACT
THE PYRAMIDS'
UNIQUE SHAPE IS
BECAUSE THEY WERE
MEANT TO LOOK LIKE A
BEAM OF LIGHT COMING
THROUGH A CLOUD.

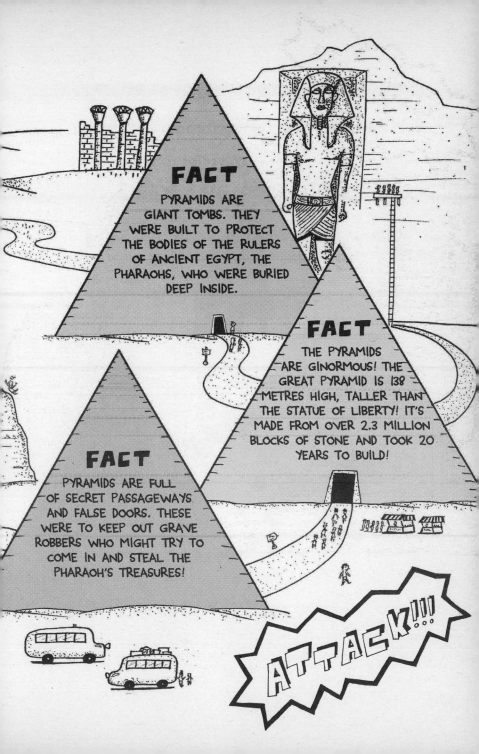

'Yikes!' said Knowledge. 'You'll never get *me* in a pyramid!'

Just then the Nerve Centre doors slid open.

CHAPTER 2
STEP BACK IN TIME

'AT LAST! CAPTAIN Fact and Knowledge,' said Professor Miniscule, the world's shortest genius. 'If you'd taken much longer *I* would have been mummified!' He pointed at his watch. 'There's no time to waste, we've an archaeologist to save!'

'As long as we don't have to go inside a pyramid,' said Knowledge nervously.

'Never mind going into a pyramid. First of all we're going to have to get you back to the time of the Ancient Egyptians,' said Professor Miniscule.

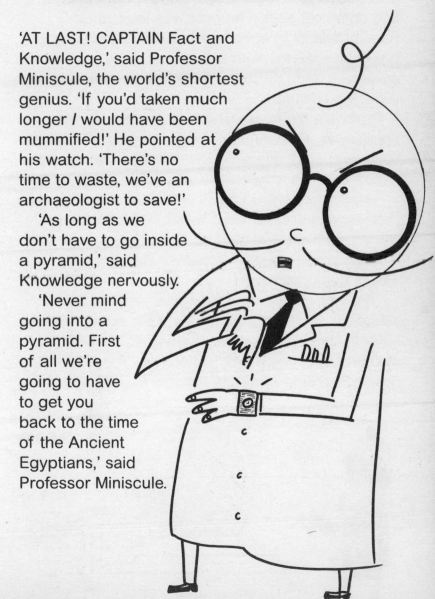

'Back in time?' gulped Captain Fact. 'Not again!'

'Yes,' said Professor Miniscule. 'Not since it was built has anyone been down this secret passage and come out alive. The only way to save Sir Ramsbottom is to send you back to Ancient Egypt. I've been tinkering with time travel since your last adventure and I've come up with a brand new time travelling concept.'

Professor Miniscule pressed a button on the control panel. There was a high-pitched wobbling noise and gradually a virtual doorway materialised before them.

'Gentlemen, I give you . . . the Time Portal!' said Professor Miniscule. 'Step through this and you literally step into the past.'

'Step into the past!' exclaimed Captain Fact. 'How's that possible?'

'The Time Portal liquidizes every molecule in your body, then catapults them back in time, before reconstituting them in the designated time period,' said Professor Miniscule ominously. '*Your* designated time period is Ancient Egypt 2589 BC.'

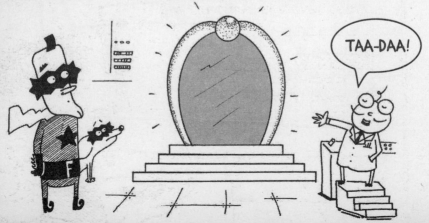

As Captain Fact and Knowledge
nervously contemplated stepping back
4,500 years, Professor Miniscule's
daughter Factorella suddenly dropped in
through the ceiling.

'When are we off, Dad? I can't wait
to get into that pyramid,' gushed
Factorella. 'The Curse of the Mummy
doesn't scare me!'

'Curse of the Mummy?' quaked
Knowledge. 'Who said anything about
a curse?'

'Ker-Fact!' piped up Captain Fact.
'When Tutankhamun's tomb was
opened in 1923, several people involved
in the excavation died in mysterious
circumstances.'

'This isn't the time or the place for
Facts,' interrupted Professor Miniscule. 'And
you know you're too young to go on missions,
Factorella. I told you to programme Factotum,
the Fact Cave's Supercomputer. Now,
what have you come up with?'

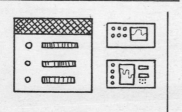

'Thanks Factorella. Now, haven't you got homework to do?' asked Professor Miniscule. 'I've got to set the Time Portal to 2589 BC.'

As Professor Miniscule fiddled with the date setting on the Time Portal, Factorella sidled up to Captain Fact.

'Psst! You might find this useful,' she said, slipping him a rolled-up piece of paper.

'Factorella, I thought I told you to go to your room,' barked Professor Miniscule. 'Any more nonsense from you and you're grounded!'

As Factorella sloped off, Captain Fact unrolled the piece of paper.

It was a hand-drawn map of Egypt . . .

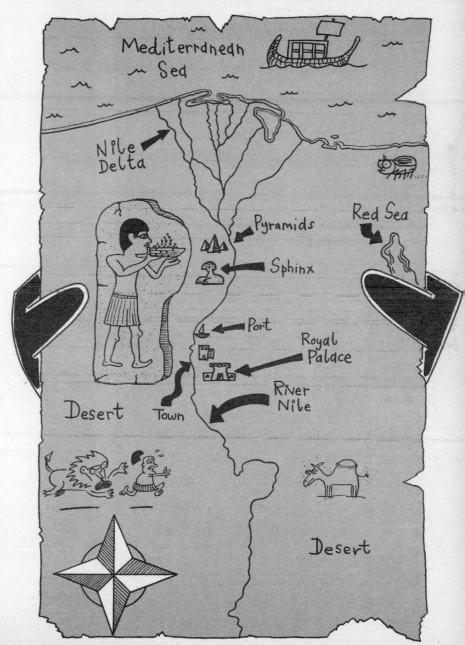

'The Time Portal is now primed for Ancient Egypt,' declared Professor Miniscule. 'Let's just hope you don't step out into something nasty, like a battle or a plague.'

'A plague?' whimpered Knowledge. But there was no turning back.

'Good luck gentlemen,' said Professor Miniscule, 'and prepare to say "Hello Pharaoh"!'

Captain Fact and Knowledge stepped through the Time Portal.

SECRET FACT!

SO HOW DO WE KNOW THAT FACTORELLA WILL GROW UP TO BE A SUPERHERO?

EVEN AS A BABY FACTORELLA STOOD OUT FROM THE CROWD!

GOO-GOO!

GA-GA!

CONSTELLATION!

WHEN HER FRIENDS WERE LEARNING TO WALK SHE COULD ALREADY JUGGLE, FIRE BREATHE AND DO THE TRAPEZE - AT THE SAME TIME!

AND A FEW YEARS LATER, WHILE THE OTHER KIDS WERE OUTSIDE RIDING THEIR BIKES, FACTORELLA WAS INDOORS TURBOCHARGING HERS ...

NOW THAT FACTORELLA'S AT SCHOOL IT'S EVEN MORE OBVIOUS THAT SHE'S NOT LIKE THE OTHER CHILDREN . . .

SHE'S EVEN BEEN BANNED FROM SCHOOL SPORTS DAY . . .

SO IT DOESN'T TAKE A GENIUS TO SEE THAT FACTORELLA WILL GROW UP TO BE A SUPERHERO. BUT IN THE MEANWHILE . . .

CHAPTER 3
HELLO PHARAOH!

AS CAPTAIN FACT and Knowledge emerged into Ancient Egypt the Time Portal fizzled and faded behind them.

All around them were towering columns, colossal glistening granite statues and thrones inlaid with precious stones.

'That was weird,' said Knowledge, still recovering from the time travel. 'It was like gargling a giant fizzy drink and having my toes tickled by a thousand ants, all at the same time.'

'Shh, Knowledge,' whispered Captain Fact. 'It looks like we're in some sort of Royal Palace. And look, there's the Pharaoh!'

'Why are all these people on their hands and knees?' asked Knowledge. 'Has the Pharaoh lost a contact lens?'

'Don't be ridiculous, Knowledge,' said Captain Fact. 'Ker-Fact! The Pharaoh's subjects would kiss the ground before him as a mark of respect. We seem to have stumbled into some sort of special occasion.'

'Special occasion?' said Knowledge cheerfully. 'Great! Do you think there will be dancing? Or Pass the Parcel? I love special occasions.'

'I think you'll find we haven't been invited to *this* special occasion,' said Captain Fact. 'And we've got a pyramid puzzle to solve. This place is crawling with guards – let's get out of here.'

Captain Fact and Knowledge tried and tried to find a way out of the Palace. They ran through corridors, down stairs, past arches and around columns. Everywhere was bustling with people. 'The Pharaoh must be very popular,' said Knowledge. 'We've never had this many friends to stay.'

'They're not friends,' said Captain Fact. 'Ker-Fact! The Palace is more like a headquarters than a home. All of these people help to run Egypt.'

Narrowly avoiding yet more guards they found themselves in the Royal Kitchen.

'I'm starting to like Ancient Egypt,' said Knowledge, licking his lips. All around them were tables groaning with the finest Egyptian foods: dates, figs, cucumbers, melons, pomegranates, grapes, jars of honey.

'There's no time for that, Knowledge!' said Captain Fact, sternly. 'I've got a plan – we're going to hide in these empty wine jars and sit tight for a while.'

'I'd love to have been a Pharaoh,' whispered Knowledge. 'People on their hands and knees, loads of great grub . . .'

'Not to mention all the fabulous gifts from visitors to the court,' said Captain Fact, as his head began to throb . . .

All of a sudden they felt themselves being lifted up . . .

'What's going on?' whispered Knowledge.

'With any luck my plan's working and we're being carried out of the Palace,' said Captain Fact. Sure enough a pair of burly Egyptians had heaved the wine jars containing our two superheroes onto their shoulders and were carrying them out into the town.

CHAPTER 4
WALK LIKE AN EGYPTIAN

EVENTUALLY THE JARS containing Captain Fact and Knowledge were dumped in the back yard of a shop.

'We've done it, we're out of the Palace!' cried Captain Fact, wringing out his cape. 'Now all we've got to do is find a boat.'

'A boat?' asked Knowledge, flicking wine from his tail, 'I thought we were surrounded by desert.'

'We are,' said Captain Fact, 'but the best way to get around Egypt is on the river Nile. We've got to get to the Great Pyramid, we've an archaeologist to save!'

Just then the shop
owner appeared. The
last thing he was expecting
to see was a superhero and a
talking dog.

He shouted angrily at them in
Ancient Egyptian and chased
after them with a broom.

'I don't think the locals are
too keen to meet us,' said
Captain Fact urgently. 'Let's
get out of here.'

As soon as Captain Fact and Knowledge emerged onto the street they realised that everyone was staring at them.

'We're going to need a disguise,' whispered Captain Fact. 'Let's get off the main road.'

They took the first turning off the main street and found themselves in a dusty, deserted back alley.

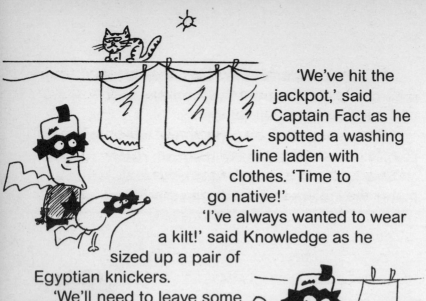

'We've hit the jackpot,' said Captain Fact as he spotted a washing line laden with clothes. 'Time to go native!'

'I've always wanted to wear a kilt!' said Knowledge as he sized up a pair of Egyptian knickers.

'We'll need to leave some sort of payment,' said Captain Fact, slipping into a linen loin cloth. 'Have you got any dog biscuits?'

'Only a couple of bags,' whined Knowledge. 'Can't you leave the Fact Watch?'

'The Fact Watch? You know I can't leave that,' said Captain Fact. 'It's our only contact with home.'

Knowledge reluctantly handed over a bag of his favourite butterscotch-flavoured doggie snacks.

With their superhero outfits safely stashed under Captain Fact's headdress, they were now walking unnoticed among the locals.

'Time to use that map Factorella gave us,' said Captain Fact. 'Right, Knowledge, if I'm not badly mistaken the Nile is due west of us.'

As they followed Factorella's map, they couldn't help but be amazed by the bustling, humming streets around them.

'What an incredible place,' whispered Knowledge. 'I thought people would be living in huts and chasing lions.'

'Not in Ancient Egypt. This was one of the great civilisations of the world,' said Captain Fact, as his ears began to wobble . . .

Suddenly there it was before them, just where Factorella had shown it on the map, the mighty river Nile.

'Here it is, Knowledge,' said Captain Fact. 'Ancient Egypt's motorway, a multi-laned expressway joining north and south!'

CHAPTER 5
NILE BE BACK

'RIGHT, KNOWLEDGE,' SAID Captain Fact. 'The pyramids are downstream from here. We're going to have to get onto a boat.'

'Great, and I've seen just the one for us,' said Knowledge pointing at a lavish, golden vessel. 'Look, they've got music, an on-board buffet, belly dancers . . .'

'Ker-Fact! Ancient Egyptians were the first people to have tourism,' said Captain Fact. 'The wealthy used to take pleasure cruises up the Nile!'

'Dinner at the Captain's table . . . I can't wait,' said Knowledge, about to board the luxurious liner.

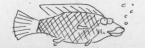

'Stop right there, Knowledge,' said Captain Fact. 'We're meant to be undercover, remember. We're going to have to sneak onto a boat and hide until we get to the Great Pyramid. And *I've* spotted the very one!'

A herd of cows was being led up a wobbly gangplank and onto the deck of a battered old cattle barge. Swarms of flies buzzed around and the air was heavy with the stench of cow dung.

'Grab a cow and hold on tight!' said Captain Fact.

Once onboard, Captain Fact and Knowledge found themselves penned in with dozens of mooing cows.

'I'm up to my knees in a cow pat,' moaned Knowledge, pinching his nose.

'Don't worry, Knowledge, we should be there in no time,' said Captain Fact as the boat creaked into action.

'I hope so,' said Knowledge. 'If I get another hoof on my paw . . .'

'The Nile's amazing, Knowledge,' said Captain Fact. 'Did you know it's the longest river in the world? Without it there would have been no Ancient Egypt.' And with that his toes began to tingle . . .

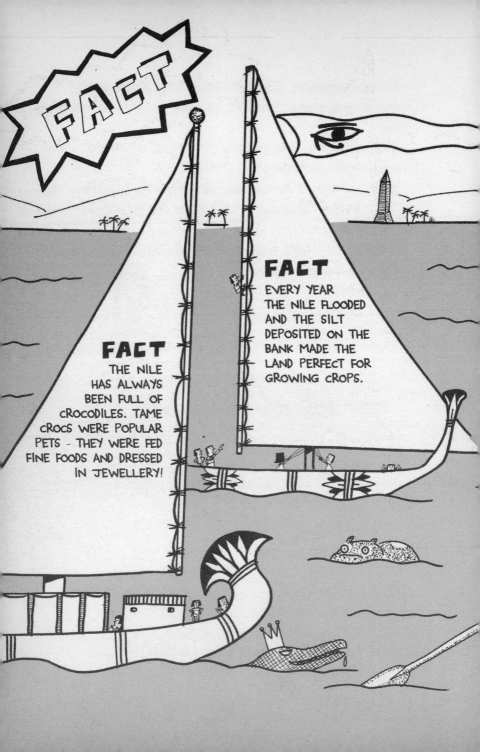

When the boat finally docked Captain Fact and Knowledge found themselves back on dry land.

'I thought we'd be closer to the pyramids,' said Knowledge as he squinted at the horizon.

'So did I. According to the map they're straight ahead,' said Captain Fact. 'We'd better start walking.'

As Captain Fact and Knowledge set out on the final part of their journey across the desert to the pyramids, there was a thunderous rumbling and all around them the ground began to shake.

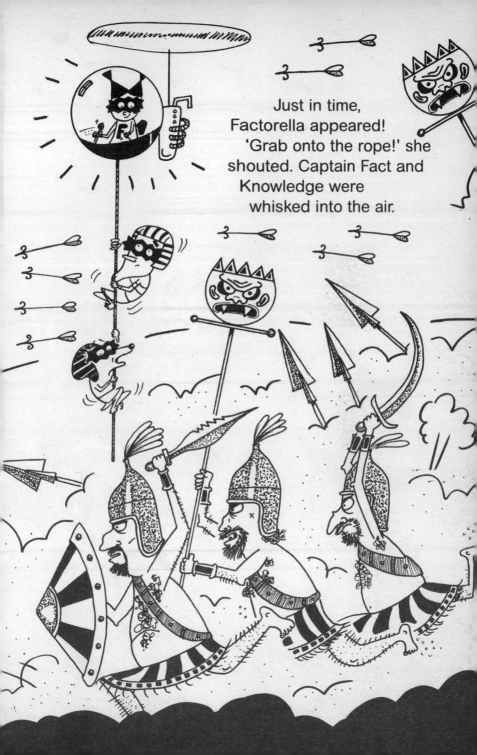

Just in time,
Factorella appeared!
'Grab onto the rope!' she
shouted. Captain Fact and
Knowledge were
whisked into the air.

'What do you think of the TimeCopter, guys?' asked Factorella as they pulled away from the battle raging below.

'Brilliant,' said Captain Fact. 'Can we have one?'

''Fraid not,' said Factorella, 'it's just a prototype. Dad only let me use it because it was an emergency.'

The TimeCopter gently landed by a herd of camels.

'Catch a camel and head north,' said Factorella. 'I'd love to stay, but I've got to get back to do the washing up.'

'Thanks, Factorella,' said Captain Fact, waving as the TimeCopter disappeared with a loud bang.

CHAPTER 6
SPHINX JINX

WITH THEIR CAMEL charging along at top speed it wasn't long before the pyramids were within reach.

'Almost there, Knowledge,' said Captain Fact as he surveyed the fast approaching monuments.

'And look, there's a welcoming committee out to meet us!' said Knowledge as a large group of sweating Egyptian builders came into view.

'I don't think they're a welcoming committee,' said Captain Fact as the camel came to a halt. All around them was a frenzy of activity, a blur of workmen and tools.

As Captain Fact and Knowledge dismounted, chisels and wooden mallets were thrust into their hands and they were pointed in the direction of a giant sculpture.

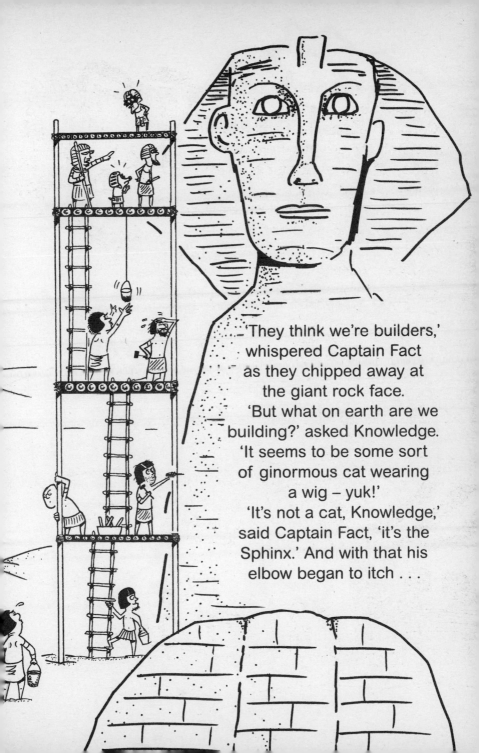

'They think we're builders,'
whispered Captain Fact
as they chipped away at
the giant rock face.
'But what on earth are we
building?' asked Knowledge.
'It seems to be some sort
of ginormous cat wearing
a wig – yuk!'
'It's not a cat, Knowledge,'
said Captain Fact, 'it's the
Sphinx.' And with that his
elbow began to itch . . .

FACT
THE GREAT SPHINX IS A HUGE STATUE WITH THE BODY OF A LION AND THE HEAD OF A PHARAOH.

FACT
THE SPHINX IS CARVED FROM A SOLID BLOCK OF LIMESTONE! IT'S 57 METRES LONG AND 20 METRES HIGH: THAT'S HALF AS LONG AS A FOOTBALL PITCH AND TALLER THAN A HOUSE!

FACT
THE EGYPTIANS USED STATUES OF LIONS TO GUARD IMPORTANT BUILDINGS. THE GREAT SPHINX WAS PROBABLY MEANT TO GUARD THE GREAT PYRAMID.

In the distance a bell was ringing and all around them the workers were downing their tools.

'Must be some sort of Egyptian tea break,' whispered Captain Fact.

He and Knowledge joined the builders, who were busy tucking into their break-time snack of honey-cakes and figs.

'Being a worker in Ancient Egypt isn't so bad,' said Knowledge, guzzling his way through his fifteenth fig.

'Don't get too cosy, Knowledge, we've got an archaeologist to save,' said Captain Fact, as the bell sounded again for the end of break-time.

As the workmen returned to their posts Captain
Fact saw their opportunity.

'Quick, Knowledge, jump on to this sledge,' said
Captain Fact. 'It's our ticket out of here.' As Captain
Fact and Knowledge perched on the pile of rubble
it slowly began to lurch forward.

'We're being pulled out of the building site
towards a dump,' said Captain Fact. 'We'll hop off
when we pass the pyramids.'

'OK, Knowledge, NOW!' said Captain Fact leaping from the sledge.

'There's three of them!' said Knowledge, dusting himself down.

'Yes,' said Captain Fact. 'Ker-fact! There's the Pyramid of Mycerinus, the Pyramid of Chephren and the one we want: the Great Pyramid of Cheops.'

'Great, said Knowledge. 'Let's just pop in, find the secret tunnel and be home for dinner.'

'It's not going to be that easy,' said Captain Fact. 'Pyramids don't have front doors. It's time to use the Power of Fact . . .'

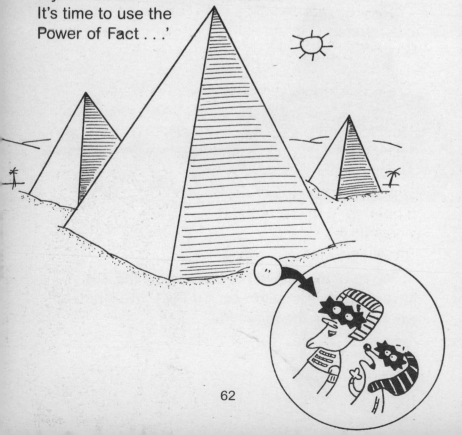

62

CHAPTER 7
WRAP STARS

'WHAT DO YOU find in the middle of a pyramid?' asked Captain Fact.

'Jam?' suggested Knowledge.

'No, no, Knowledge,' said Captain Fact. 'Mummies. And how do you think they get into the pyramid?'

'Well my mummy likes to take the bus,' said Knowledge.

'They get carried in by the High Priests,' said an exasperated Captain Fact. 'That means if *we* get mummified, they'll carry *us* in! To the Embalming Hall!'

'Embalming Hall?' quavered Knowledge.

'Yes, it's right next to the pyramid,' said Captain Fact. 'It's where mummification takes place.'

Ducking past guards and avoiding look-out posts, Captain Fact and Knowledge slipped in to the forbidding gloom of the Embalming Hall.

'Looks like they're preparing to mummify someone,' said Captain Fact. All around them knives were being sharpened and ointments prepared.

'Why is one of them in fancy dress?'
gulped Knowledge.

'He's the High Priest,' said Captain Fact, 'and
that's not fancy dress. That mask depicts Anubis,
one of the gods of the Ancient Egyptians.' And with
that his nose began to twitch . . .

A hush descended as a body was carried in and placed on the marble embalming table.

'This is going to get gory,' said Captain Fact excitedly.

'What are they sticking up his nose?' asked Knowledge.

'That's a brain hook,' said Captain Fact. 'It's inserted up the nose to scoop out the brain!'

Next the High Priest brandished a golden knife. . .

'What's he going to chop off?' whimpered Knowledge.

'Oh he's not chopping anything off,' said Captain Fact, 'he's going to make a cut on the side of the body and remove its internal organs!'

The High Priest then produced a bottle of wine.

'Phew, after all that I'm not surprised he wants a lovely glass of wine,' sighed Knowledge.

'He's not going to drink it,' said Captain Fact. 'Wine is used to rinse out the body. It's then covered in a salt called natron to preserve it. Only then is it wrapped in bandages.'

As the High Priest completed the mummifying procedure the newly mummified body was held aloft. With great ceremony it was carefully placed into a sparkling gold sarcophagus and the lid scraped shut.

As Knowledge slumped into a queasy heap, Captain Fact's eyes began to glow . . .

As the High Priests and their assistants filed out of the hall, Captain Fact seized the moment. Grabbing two lengths of bandage he started winding them around Knowledge's paws.

'What are you doing?' asked Knowledge. 'I don't remember asking for first aid.'

'It's not first aid,' said Captain Fact, 'we're getting mummified.'

CHAPTER 8
BURIED ALIVE!

BANDAGED UP TO the ears, Captain Fact and
Knowledge waddled over to the mummy
and carefully placed themselves
amongst the glittering
funeral items.

LISTEN UP!

'Right, Knowledge,' whispered Captain Fact,
'here's the plan. Any minute now the priests are
going to bury the mummy and all his belongings in
the pyramid's secret chamber. They're going to
think we're part of his possessions and bury us
too! We'll be taken right to the very same chamber
where Sir Ramsbottom is trapped 4,500 years from
now! Hand over that last bag of doggie biscuits.'
    Just then the room filled with the funeral
procession and Captain Fact and Knowledge were
swept up and carried off.

'We're being carried along the secret passage,' whispered Captain Fact as he started to sprinkle doggie biscuits behind them.

'What are you doing with my snacks?' asked Knowledge. 'How can you be so disrespectful? They're pineapple-chunk flavour!'

'I'm leaving a trail,' said Captain Fact.

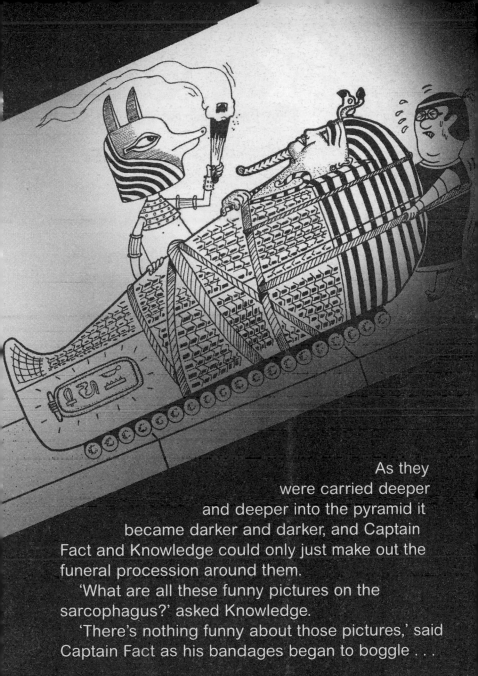

As they
were carried deeper
and deeper into the pyramid it
became darker and darker, and Captain
Fact and Knowledge could only just make out the
funeral procession around them.

'What are all these funny pictures on the
sarcophagus?' asked Knowledge.

'There's nothing funny about those pictures,' said
Captain Fact as his bandages began to boggle . . .

FACT

ANCIENT EGYPTIAN WRITING IS CALLED HIEROGLYPHICS. INSTEAD OF LETTERS IT USES PICTURES, OR 'HIEROGLYPHS', OF WHICH THERE WERE MORE THAN 700!

FACT

HIEROGLYPHS REPRESENT DIFFERENT SOUNDS OR OBJECTS. THE SHAPES WERE BASED ON EVERYDAY THINGS FOUND IN ANCIENT EGYPT LIKE OWLS, DUCKS AND WATER.

FACT

FOR CENTURIES NO ONE COULD UNDERSTAND HIEROGLYPHICS. BUT IN 1799 THE ROSETTA STONE WAS DISCOVERED. IT HAD A TEXT IN THREE LANGUAGES, ONE OF WHICH WAS ANCIENT GREEK AND ANOTHER HIEROGLYPHICS - BY COMPARING THE TWO THE CODE WAS CRACKED!

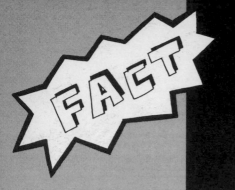

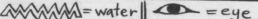 

= water   = eye   = tre

ATTACK!!!

FACT

BECAUSE HIEROGLYPHICS WERE SO COMPLICATED HARDLY ANYONE COULD READ OR WRITE. THIS MEANT SCRIBES WERE HIGHLY PRIZED. IT TOOK FIVE YEARS' TRAINING, AND YOU STARTED AT THE AGE OF NINE!

FACT

ANCIENT EGYPTIANS WROTE ON PAPYRUS, WHICH IS A REED THAT GROWS BY THE NILE. STRIPS WERE BEATEN AND WOVEN TO MAKE PAPER.

= snake   = star   = night

After being carried through increasingly narrow passages and ever steepening staircases the procession finally arrived in the secret burial chamber.

'Thank goodness we're here,' whispered Captain Fact. 'That was the last dog biscuit.'

Captain Fact and Knowledge were carefully placed in the chamber alongside the mummy and its hoard of possessions. After the funeral party left there was a deep rumbling as a giant granite slab shuddered across the entrance.

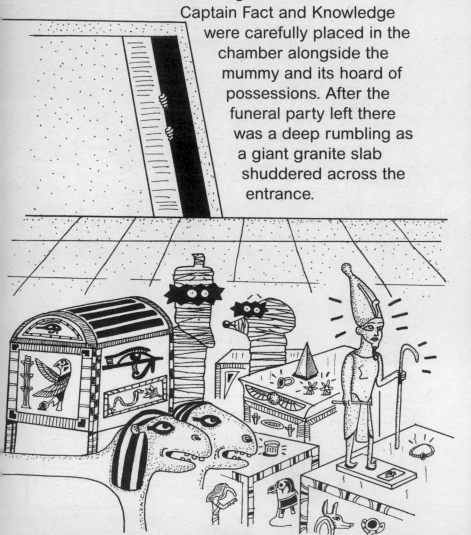

'We're sealed in,' said Captain Fact. 'That wasn't part of the plan.'

LOOK AT ALL THESE WONDERFUL THINGS!

All around them were piles of offerings.

'We seem to be trapped in a furniture shop,' said Knowledge. 'Look, there's beds, stools, cabinets, chairs . . .'

'There must be something in here we can use to get out,' said Captain Fact rummaging through the treasures. But just then his toes began to tingle . . .

FACT

FOR ALL YOUR

TOYS

YOU'LL NEVER GET BORED IN THE AFTERLIFE WITH A BOARD GAME. NEW IN EBONY AND IVORY, ANCIENT EGYPT'S MOST POPULAR BOARD GAME: 'SENET'.

MAKE-UP

WHEN YOU MEET YOUR ANCESTORS IN THE AFTERLIFE, YOU'RE GOING TO WANT TO LOOK YOUR BEST. SO MAKE SURE YOU HAVE MAKE-UP BOXES AND MIRRORS.

SERVANTS

WHO WANTS TO WORK WHEN THEY'RE DEAD? NO ONE, SO TA_ SOME MODELS OF SERVANTS. THEY'LL COME TO LIFE WH_ YOU'RE DEAD AND DO ALL YOUR WORK FOR YOU!

AFTERLIFE NEEDS!

FOOD & DRINK

THE AFTERLIFE CAN BE A THIRSTY PLACE, SO MAKE SURE YOU PACK THIS MODEL OF A BREWER. YOU'LL THEN BE ABLE TO DRINK BEER FOR ETERNITY!

MUSICAL INSTRUMENTS

FILL THE AFTERLIFE WITH SOUND WITH ONE OF OUR WONDERFUL MUSICAL INSTRUMENTS. WE'VE GOT HARPS, FLUTES AND RATTLES!

ATTACK!!!

After much rummaging Captain Fact emerged
with a ceremonial spear.

'Grab one of these, Knowledge, and pull,' said
Captain Fact. The two of them set about trying to
dislodge the granite slab.

CHAPTER 9
CURSE OF THE MUMMY!

AFTER A LOT of puffing and panting Captain Fact and Knowledge finally inched back the giant granite block, just enough to allow them to squeeze through.

'What's that noise?' asked Captain Fact, unbandaging his head. 'I'm sure I heard a munching sound.'

Knowledge was already tucking in to the first dog biscuit of their trail.

'It's nervous eating,' pleaded Knowledge. 'This place gives me the creeps.'

'Well, if we follow the trail of dog biscuits we should be out in no time,' said Captain Fact. 'You lead the way and I'll log our coordinates into the Fact Watch. As soon as we're out we'll relay the information to Professor Miniscule and he can make a map to save Sir Ramsbottom.'

And so with Knowledge frantically munching dog biscuits and Captain Fact frantically tracking their course, our two superheroes undertook the death defying task of exiting the pyramid in one piece. Everywhere there were traps and false entrances . . .

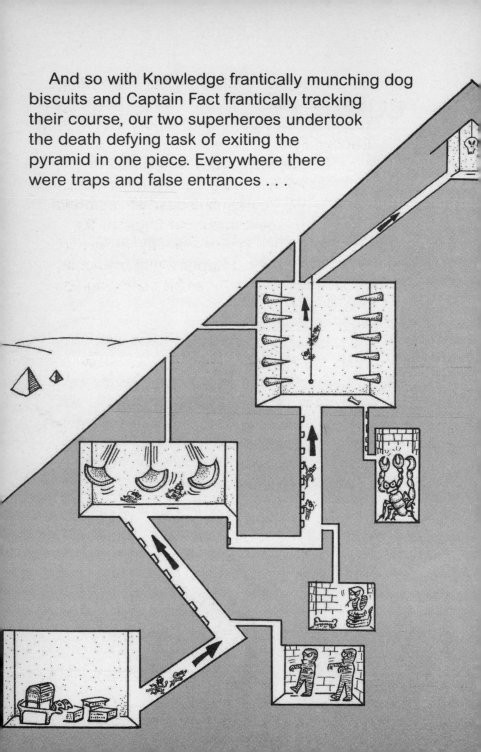

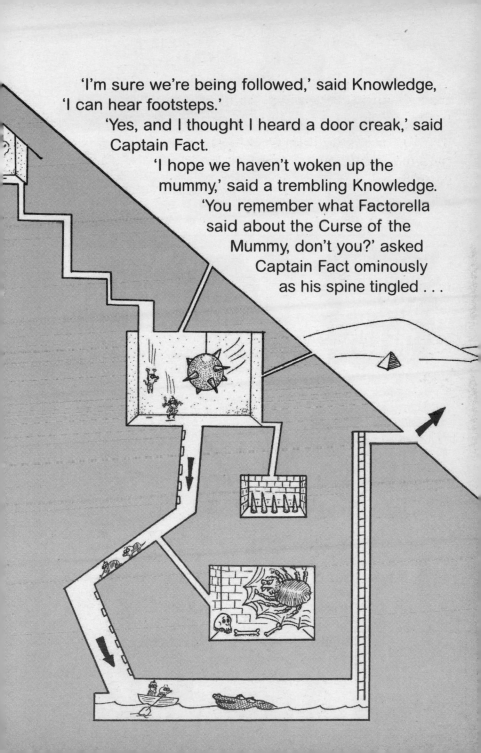

'I'm sure we're being followed,' said Knowledge, 'I can hear footsteps.'

'Yes, and I thought I heard a door creak,' said Captain Fact.

'I hope we haven't woken up the mummy,' said a trembling Knowledge.

'You remember what Factorella said about the Curse of the Mummy, don't you?' asked Captain Fact ominously as his spine tingled . . .

FACT

REX CINEMA MUMMY SEASON

TOMB *With A View*

"THEY WHO ENTER THIS SACRED TOMB SHALL BE VISITED BY THE WINGS OF DEATH!" NEWSPAPERS CLAIMED THAT THIS WAS WRITTEN OUTSIDE TUTANKHAMUN'S TOMB, BUT THE REPORTERS HAD MADE IT UP!

MUMMY I SHRANK THE KIDS

HOWARD CARTER WAS IN CHARGE OF THE EXPEDITION. WHEN HE ENTERED THE TOMB HIS PET CANARY WAS KILLED BY A COBRA. THE COBRA WAS THE SYMBOL OF THE PHARAOH!

ATTACK of the ALIEN MUMMIES

LORD CARNARVON, THE MAN WHO PAID FOR THE EXPEDITION TO FIND TUTANKHAMUN, DIED FOUR MONTHS AFTER HE ENTERED THE TOMB!

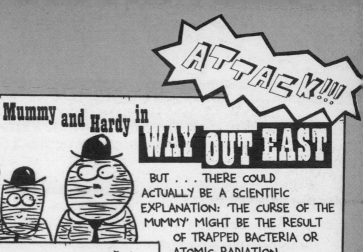

ATTACK!!!...

Mummy and Hardy in WAY OUT EAST

BUT . . . THERE COULD ACTUALLY BE A SCIENTIFIC EXPLANATION: 'THE CURSE OF THE MUMMY' MIGHT BE THE RESULT OF TRAPPED BACTERIA OR ATOMIC RADIATION RELEASED WHEN THE TOMB WAS OPENED. NOT ONLY THAT, BUT MOST DEATHS RELATING TO THE TOMB CAN BE EXPLAINED AND HOWARD CARTER HIMSELF LIVED TO A RIPE OLD AGE!

MUMMY FROM THE BLACK LAGOON

LORD CARNARVON DIED FROM A MOSQUITO BITE THAT WENT SEPTIC. TUTANKHAMUN'S MUMMY HAD A SCAR ON HIS FACE IN EXACTLY THE SAME PLACE!

TICKETS

Finally Captain Fact and Knowledge could see a chink of daylight.

'We've done it!' said Captain Fact as they stumbled blinking into the bright sunlight. 'I feel amazing!'

'And I feel stuffed,' burped Knowledge.

But Captain Fact wasn't listening as they dashed down the side of the pyramid. At the bottom, Captain Fact once again turned to the Fact Watch to make contact with Professor Miniscule.

YIPPEEE!

'Come in, Professor Miniscule – do you read me?' he said.

'Loud and clear, Captain Fact,' crackled Professor Miniscule. 'Congratulations! You've solved the Mystery of the Secret Passage!'

'We wouldn't have done it without Knowledge's dog biscuits,' said Captain Fact.

'Well, those dog biscuits have saved the world's leading archaeologist,' said Professor Miniscule. 'I've downloaded your coordinates and as we speak a map is being sent to the Egyptian authorities.'

All of a sudden there was a loud wobbling noise and a doorway started to shimmer in the distance.

'The Time Portal should be stabilising,' said Professor Miniscule, 'I've set it so you return to your office in time for the evening weather forecast.'
Captain Fact and Knowledge took a final long look at the splendour of Ancient Egypt before stepping back through the Time Portal.

CHAPTER 10
AND NOW THE WEATHER . . .

UNFORTUNATELY THE TIME Portal was a little bit off beam. Rather than stepping out into their office, Captain Fact and Knowledge stepped out into the office gym and only just got their masks off in time.

As the Boss looked up from his exercise bike he couldn't believe his eyes. 'I'm sure I just saw Thornhill and Puddles dressed as mummies,' gasped the Boss, rubbing his eyes, 'I knew exercise wasn't good for you. I'm taking the rest of the day off!'

Cliff and Puddles were already sprinting to their office to get changed.

Fresh out of their bandages Cliff and Puddles dashed into the Make-up Department.

'There you are, Cliff, I've been looking all over for you,' said Lucy. 'Captain Fact's done it again! Look, it's coming up on the news now.'

Cliff, Puddles and Lucy all looked up at the TV monitor where a recently rescued Sir Ramsbottom was being interviewed.

THANKS TO CAPTAIN FACT'S MAP I WAS ABLE TO GET OUT OF THE PYRAMID. NOT ONLY THAT BUT I MADE AN EXTRAORDINARY DISCOVERY - ANCIENT EGYPTIAN DOG BISCUITS.

'I think Sir Ramsbottom's hot,' said Lucy, 'but not as hot as Captain Fact. I'd like to be entombed in a pyramid with *him!*'

Cliff blushed as he and Puddles stepped under the studio lights and in front of the cameras.

And so with Sir Ramsbottom safely back in his favourite museum, Cliff Thornhill and Puddles were back doing what they did worst – the weather.

Until the next crisis...